To Chloe, who hates cabbages.

Published by Caroline House
Boyds Mills Press, Inc.
A Highlights Company
910 Church Street
Honesdale, Pennsylvania 18431

First U.S. Edition

Library of Congress Catalog Card Number: 90-084007
ISBN: 1-878093-10-X

Printed in Hong Kong

SOMETHING NASTY in the CABBAGES

Diz Wallis

A tale from ROMAN DE RENARD
written in the 12th century by
Pierre de Saint-Cloud
and retold for this edition by
the artist

Caroline House

There was once, not so very long ago, a farm that was owned by Constant and his wife. Here they are, looking cross. Next to the farmyard was a cabbage patch, where the hens lived, and here they would strut and scratch and peck, fat and content, amongst the cabbages. They were quite safe from all intruders because Constant had built a solid fence with high oak stakes and sharp hawthorn. This made a barrier so tight and prickly that even the leanest, hungriest fox could not squeeze through.

There never were such happy hens. . . .

Now here is someone who knew the hens well, and his name is Reynard. The sight of the plump hens made his mouth water, for he was always famished. Yet he knew he could not catch them because of the spiky barrier that stood in his way. So he would run round and round it, jumping up and lying down, craning his neck to see if there might be some way he could break in.

Imagine, then, his pleasure when one day he found a broken stake. He couldn't believe his luck. He scrambled over and dropped quietly down into the cabbages on the other side.

At this moment proud Chantecler, the cockerel, was dozing on the dung heap in the corner of the cabbage patch. One eye was closed and one eye was open, for he had to keep guard over the hens. He felt this was his duty, even when he was asleep.

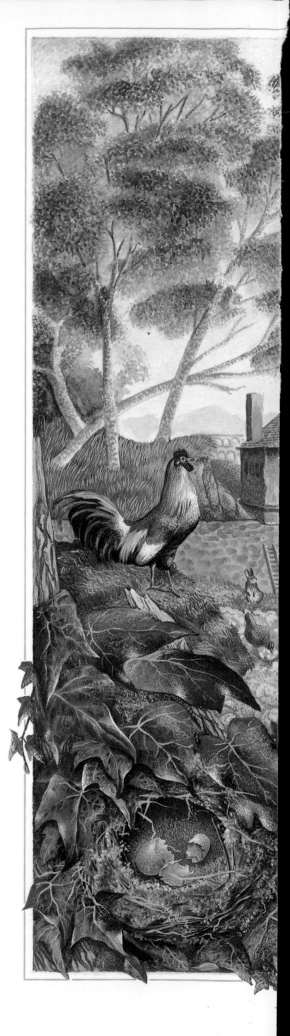

Suddenly there was a flurry of feathers and much squawking and chattering, and all the hens rushed towards Chantecler.

"Whatever is the matter?" he crowed at them.

"We saw the fence shake," they squawked. "We saw the cabbage leaves tremble. Some horrid, hungry beast is hiding amongst the cabbages, waiting to eat us all."

"Pooh! Monsters amongst cabbages, whatever next? You silly birds, nothing could get in here without my seeing it. Go back and feed." And Chantecler dismissed them all with a shake of his glossy feathers.

But something had got in. . . .

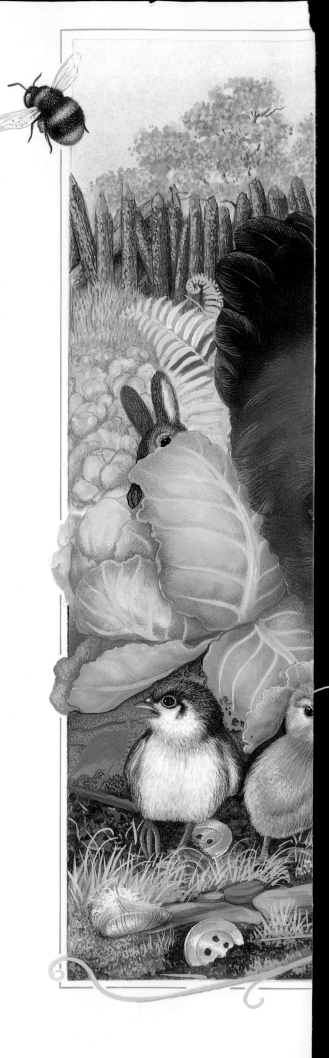

The sunlight on the steaming heap sent the cockerel back to sleep again. This time he had a dreadful dream. Something nasty was out there in the cabbages. It crept up softly, slowly, dragging behind it a red fur coat with a bone collar. It flung this pelt round poor old Chantecler, tying him up so tightly in it that he thought he might die. As soon as he awoke, though his legs shuddered and his crest shook, he hurried over to where the hens were hiding and told them all about it.

"Oh! Layers of enormous eggs! Tell me what it means," he begged.

"This coat," they said, "is a fox's coat, and the collar of bone, its teeth. Teeth that will seize and swallow you, unless you run and hide. He's out there now. Hide, Chantecler." But Chantecler was already feeling braver. "Huh! Hide? What, me? . . . No fear. I can take care of myself!" he crowed.

Oh proud and foolish bird!

Puffed up with pride at his own importance, he made his way back to his noble perch. Before long he began to nod off again, quite unaware of what was creeping up, crawling up underneath the cabbages!

Barely a leaf twitched, scarcely a twig cracked, for a fox is the king of stealth. His eyes glinted in the shadows, and when Chantecler seemed fast asleep, he pounced. But the cockerel spotted him at the last moment and sprang out of the way and up the mound. With relief, he crowed as loudly as he could, "Cock-a-doodle-doo!"

The fox was vexed, but he didn't show it. He stood at the foot of the dung heap as if spellbound. "What a magnificent voice you have! It's almost as good as your father's, but he used to close his eyes to sing. It helped him to reach those higher notes. Won't you try it?"

Chantecler was suspicious, but he wanted to prove he could outsing anyone. So he closed one eye and crowed, keeping the other firmly fixed upon the fox.

"Almost," said Reynard in a charming voice, "but to reach the very highest note, you must close both. Come a little closer and sing to me again." So Chantecler, flattered and convinced, did as he was told, closed both his eyes and sang!

Reynard, seizing the chance, fell upon the bird and carried him off, leaving but a feather or two to flutter down upon the mound.

"Didn't we tell you so?" wailed the hens in the distance. "How you mocked us and scoffed at us and wouldn't listen. Now see where your pride has got you." But fox and cockerel were already over the fence and out of earshot.

Just then the farmer's wife came to the gate to call her hens in for the night. They didn't come, and she felt uneasy. Then she saw what had happened—the fox had made off with her cockerel. She called for Constant, who ran to her side. "That wretch Reynard has made off with my Chantecler!" she screeched at him.

"Well, why didn't you stop him?" he yelled.

"Stop him? Stop him? Do you think he was waiting for me, you fool?" she snapped back at him.

Constant was wild with temper and stamped his foot and called his dogs and all his men, and off they went, with sticks and staves and hoes and rakes. Dogs barked, pigs squealed, and cats, ducks, geese, and dust flew up in all directions.

The air was full with cries of "Over here!", "This way!", "That way!", "Over there!", and "Curse the rogue!", "Catch him!", and "Tally-ho!"

The fox leapt hedges, ditches, and dikes. Now Chantecler was almost lost. He hadn't got a lot of brain, but what he had he must use now. "Friend," he croaked, "you hear those dreadful things they are shouting? Why not hurl back an insult of your own? Show them who is master hereabouts. That'll make them mad."

And Reynard, wise though he was, could not resist, for he was cunning, he was clever, but he was also very pleased with himself.

As he opened his mouth to taunt them, out flew the squawking, tattered cockerel up into the pear tree that stood nearby, leaving Reynard aghast beneath him.

"Well now, friend," crowed Chantecler, "what have you got to say to that?"

"Nothing!" snapped Reynard, who could hardly speak through fury. "But . . . but . . . oh, beware a mouth that opens when it should stay shut."

"Mmm," replied Chantecler, in deepest thought, "and may I say it? Beware an eye that shuts when it should stay open!"

So Chantecler had escaped. He was the worse for wear but wiser, and when he was back in the farmyard, he boasted to all who would listen, in a loud crowing voice, all about his great adventure and how he had foiled the fox.

And as for Reynard? Well, he was wiser, too—but he was still hungry!

The End